A WASTELAND OF MY GOD'S OWN MAKING

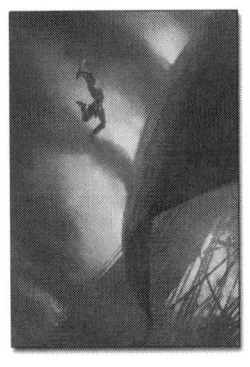

BRADLEY BEAULIEU

First Edition: February 2019

ISBN: 978-1-93964-932-4 (Paperback)
ISBN: 978-1-93964-930-0 (epub)
ISBN: 978-1-93964-931-7 (Kindle)

Please visit me on the web at
http://www.quillings.com

A WASTELAND OF MY GOD'S OWN MAKING

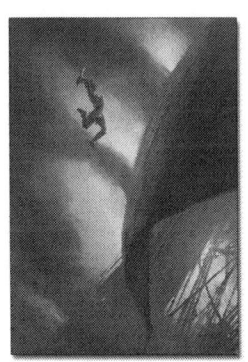

As the sun broke above the horizon, Djaga Akoyo rushed from the heavily shadowed streets into the entrance hall of the collegium medicum. The streets were cool from the chill desert night, but this place was frigid, a feeling that seeped deep below Djaga's skin, making her quicken her pace all the more.

"May I help?" An attendant—from the looks of him a scholar fresh from receiving his laurel crown—strode toward her, calm as a wading heron. When he saw the dried blood caked along the front of her beaten leather armor, however, his eyes went wide as the moons. "Oh!" was all he said.

"Calm yourself," Djaga told him. "It isn't mine."

Not all of it, in any case. "A woman name Nadín was taken here yesterday. A stab wound to the gut. Where is she?"

The young man opened his mouth, but nothing came out. "I've only just arrived."

"Well, go find her!" Djaga shouted.

"I'll take her, Ari." A tall, black-skinned woman had exited the hallway ahead of them, a high physic named Malanga. She had striking eyes and a pretty smile. The wheat-colored robes she wore was the preferred uniform in the collegium medicum, yet it seemed chosen to match her lustrous black hair, which was braided into a beehive coil atop her head. She'd treated Djaga several times, courtesy of Djaga's more vigorous battles in the pits; she even hailed from Djaga's homeland of Kundhun, yet they'd traded no more than a bit of idle chitchat over the years. Djaga felt poor about it now.

After waving the young scholar away, Malanga motioned for Djaga to follow. To Djaga's relief, Malanga seemed to have a sense of urgency about her.

"You should be prepared," she said to Djaga as they strode swiftly along the halls, "we've done all we could, but—"

"Just tell me how much time she has left."

Djaga had known Nadín's fate from the moment she'd seen the extent of the wound to her stomach. She'd just prayed that Nadín would still be alive upon her return from the desert.

"She won't see the sunset," Malanga said. From the occupied rooms to either side of the hall issued the sounds of low conversation, coughing, moaning, or the shuffle of sandaled feet. "She's so far refused milk of the poppy in hopes that you'd return, but she is in deep pain. The longer you wait—"

"Djaga?" The voice had come from the room ahead but it sounded frail, ghostlike. "Djaga, is that you?"

Djaga swallowed before speaking softly to Malanga. "I would spare her her pain, but I must speak with her first."

"The longer you wait—" Malanga tried again.

"She must know this before she departs for the farther fields."

After a pause, Malanga nodded and left.

Djaga used tentative steps to enter the room. She turned toward the bed, and the world seemed to spin. Nadín lay there, but she looked a completely different woman. Her copper skin was pale, almost yellow. Her lips were bloodless. She seemed to have fallen in on herself, a beautiful cavern collapsed after an earthquake. Swallowing the hard knot in her throat, Djaga stepped to the bedside. She'd known this was going to happen, but to now be faced with it…

Nadín grimaced, reached one hand out. "Did you find her?"

Djaga pulled a chair close to the bedside and took Nadín's quivering hand, swathed it in her own. "Yes, I found her."

Nadín swallowed once. Twice. She licked her lips before saying, "Will you tell me?"

"Could we not speak about other things? About our days sailing your ship? Or your family we met?"

"I would know what happened." Before Djaga could say anything more, her fingers gave a squeeze, a weak gesture but surprisingly strong for a woman in her state. "And you can't deny a dying woman her last wish. Do, and you'll be cursed. You don't wish to be cursed, do you, Djaga?"

Despite all the worry roiling inside her, Djaga laughed. "No, I don't wish to be cursed." Djaga paused, her eyes brimming with tears. "Very well, my sweet. I'll tell you my tale. " She took a moment, regained herself. "I brought you here. You remember? After, I returned to the harbor with Osman, and we took your ship to the desert…"

Nadín was shaking her head. "No. All of it. I deserve that much."

Djaga nodded, resigned. "As you say…"

But where to begin? How could she tell this tale to her one true love when she'd hidden so much? *One word at a time,* her father used to say.

"It was high sun the day Afua came to Sharakhai."

On a day as hot as anyone in the city could remember, thousands gathered to watch a bout in Sharakhai's storied fighting pits. They had waited a long while already, the seat sellers charging treble the already-dear rate for bouts in the central pit. They drank of lemonade and wine. They placed money with the bet takers wandering up and down the aisles, receiving special chits for the money and the bet taken. They argued about which opponent, Djaga or Talashem, would win. All the while, their eyes drifted to the two darkened mouths of the tunnels where the combatants would soon emerge. When Pelam, the lanky master of the game, strode calmly from one of them, they rushed to their feet, threw their arms in the air, and began shouting to the oven-hot air.

Pelam, who wore long, purple robes, a bejeweled vest, and an embroidered ivory cap stained with sweat, waited for the cheer to crescendo. Only then did he raise his hands and make a tamping motion. Like a flock of skylarks landing on the banks of the Haddah, the crowd went still, but they sat with ill-contained exuberance, ready to burst into motion once more.

Pelam spread his arms wide, as if welcoming them all to his home. "You are wise, my good people." He said these words quietly, yet such was the timbre of his voice that it carried to every corner of the yawning pit. "Either that or you are gifted with the keenest foresight." He turned suddenly, sweeping his attention to another section of the choked seats. "And if not that, then surely the desert gods have shined on you this day, for you will soon bear witness to one of only two final bouts that Djaga, the Lion of Kundhun, will ever fight!"

As one, the crowd roared their appreciation. Pelam would normally go on for a time, recounting her exploits, but Djaga needed no introduction to the spectators of Sharakhai. Just as the sound began to die, Djaga emerged from the tunnel. Knowing when it was his time to be the center of attention and when it wasn't, Pelam merely flourished and arm toward her and backed away. With the sun's heat washing over her, Djaga took to the center of the pit and slowly turned, allowing the crowd to take her in.

It was a thing she did to build excitement, a slow teasing of the battle about to begin. It felt familiar as heat in the desert, and yet she hardly knew what to feel, seeing so many gathered, eager to see her trade blows, eager to see blood. Since coming to Sharakhai, she'd practically lived within these walls. If it were only a matter of her body, she stand within them and fight a while longer. She was young yet. Her nagging wounds hadn't accumulated so badly that she couldn't still scrap in the dirt with the dogs. But the bouts, the things she rummaged up within her mind to wage these battles so effectively, and for so many years, they'd become like a canker, painful to the touch. And they'd grown worse over the years, until each felt as if it would consume her.

"Take him!" A young man in the crowd rent the air before him as if opening up some imaginary enemy before him. "Open him up!"

Many spurred the young man on, but Djaga ignored him, turning her attention elsewhere to a strikingly beautiful woman sitting at the very edge of the pit's walls. Nadínamira. Nadín. A woman who'd long ago captured Djaga's heart. She sat in a seat Djaga had arranged for her long ago, to take if she so chose. She rarely did, though. She was too worried over the wounds Djaga received, the danger she was in, but she'd come today, and for that, Djaga was glad.

Like a perfect marble statue in the midst of a riot, the crowed raged around Nadín. She held Djaga's eye, smiling her worried smile. Djaga nearly broke, then, nearly allowed the worry that emanated from Nadín like rays from the sun to enter her consciousness. She regained herself a moment later, choosing instead to see only Nadín's beauty, her dark lips, her curly hair lifting every so often in the meager wind. Look any deeper and she would become lost, and that was a thing Djaga couldn't allow. Not now, so close to the end. If she were going to start a new life with Nadín, she needed the money these last two bouts would bring. They both did.

The crowd had become an undulating beast now that Pelam was announcing her opponent. "Talashem," Pelam was saying, "may be a man born of the desert tribes, but he is fresh from the killing pits of Ganahil at the edges of the Thousand Territories of Kundhun." Djaga's ears perked at this—she had been born and raised in Kundhun, after all—but the rest was lost, for the bout was near.

She paced back and forth over the dusty floor of the pit she knew so well. The shouting of the gathered crowd faded. The desert's hot wind became like to a dream. She focused on Talashem. Only on Talashem. The way his battle-kissed armor hung on his spare frame. The way he favored his right hip. The way he stared at her as if he hadn't a care in the world.

I will wipe that look from your face. I will grind it against the dirt until it's gone. You will remember this fight until your dying days.

He matched her in weight. His muscles were lithe. It made her wonder just how quick he was. Osman wouldn't have pitted her against him if he weren't a good fighter. Her opponents had always been skilled, but since the public announcement of her retirement, they had featured fighters as good as the desert had to offer.

The crowd burst into a renewed flurry as pit boys ran out in a train carrying an assortment of weapons. Talashem chose a spiked shield and a shamshir while Djaga chose one of the tall leather shields from her homeland and a heavy, curving club, its end round like a fist, studded with nails.

All the while Djaga whispered under her breath. *I*

ask not for your favor, Sjado. I ask not for your favor. I only give what you require, Sjado. I only give what you require.

As she returned to her starting point, images of the dead returned to her. Her cousin, lying on green grass, his blood bright beneath the summer sun. Her uncle not so far from him. Her brother as well. Seven others. Her family, by the gods. All of them her family.

She heard no murmur of reply. Felt no sense of favor from the god she'd invoked. But she felt Sjado's hunger. It was growing inside Djaga, as it always did when she called upon it. An old friend, it sat within her chest, crouched like a lion. It enlivened her frame, making her club feel as light as air, her shield invincible.

Nearby, Pelam struck his gong, signaling the start of the bout. Djaga strode forward.

I ask not for your favor.

Talashem moved to meet her, wary, ready.

I only give what you require.

Perhaps Talashem saw it within her. Perhaps he was simply being wary. But he backed away as Djaga charged, bringing her club down on him as Sjado's light filled her from within. That was when she felt it, a familiar sensation coming from somewhere in the crowd. It was something she hadn't felt since leaving her homeland: another who could touch Sjado. Another spurned by the two-faced god.

Afua…

Many years before that bout in the pits, far, far away from the heat of Sharakhai, a younger Djaga stood on a hill as the ceaseless winds of Kundhun swept over the grasslands.

Like standing on the shore of an emerald sea, Djaga thought.

"Come now," Afua called from the base of the hill. "Always mooning."

Afua wore a leather dress with wooden beads sewn into the shape of an orange dahlia, the sign of their tribe. She shouldered a leather bag, within which were the tools they would need to commit their crime.

"I'm not *mooning,*" Djaga replied, taking to the downward slope. "I'm admiring the beauty before me. You should try it one day."

Afua replied with a jaunty air as she headed off between two of the hills. "No time. We've *work* to do."

"Work to do…" Djaga spoke softly, the wind stealing her words. "Conspiracies to commit, more like."

Even so, she followed Afua willingly.

They soon came to a hill that was shaped differently than the rest. It looked like a spearhead, and into its narrowest slope, the place from which the spear's haft would extend, a stone door was set. Growing along the threshold and the door's surface were green moss and white lichen. Now that they were here, the worry that had seemed so far away felt close, a crow flying above her, cawing and judging, like a servant of Sjado herself.

When Afua reached into her bag and pulled from it a length of stout iron, Djaga said, "Are you sure we should do this?"

Afua shrugged, handed the iron bar to Djaga, and pulled out a second from the bag. "Is all not fair in war?"

"We are not at war." The pry bar's weight felt obscene.

"Did your father not tell you?" Afua used the tapered end of her bar to prize at the tomb's seal. "The grasslands are *always* at war."

Djaga waited, watching the way behind though she was certain they hadn't been followed. They'd come to a place that had been hidden for a hundred years. Only a handful knew anything more than the stories told around the fires, stories of warrior women who'd led the Great Reclamation of the central hills, bringing two generations of peace. *And here we are, come to steal their glory.*

No, Djaga told herself. It wasn't glory they were after, but a way to touch Sjado and Jonsu both. It wasn't for *themselves* that they had come. It was for the good of the king and queen. For the good of the tribe. War stood on the horizon. It was their duty to do all they could to prepare. Wasn't that what Djaga's father had told her growing up?

Well, here I am, Djaga spoke to his memory. *This is needed.*

"Well, put your shoulders into it," Djaga said, sick of watching Afua struggle with the seal. She took her own bar and drove it into the gap with a sharp, full-bodied thrust. When she leaned against it, powering her weight into the bar, she felt the door shift. A sigh of air was released from the tomb. It smelled of loam and decay and long-forgotten days.

They descended into darkness. Well below the surface of the barrow, lit only by the sunlight filtering in from behind them, was a stone-lined space reaching out into the darkness, until it was swallowed by the gloom. On either side of a central aisle were dozens of sarcophagi. Wreaths of withered grass and flowers lay centered on their dusty lids.

"Which one?" Djaga asked.

"To the far end," Afua replied. "The spear's tip. The place of honor."

They counted as they went, a dozen, then two, then fifty, until at last they came to the end of the great, subterranean hall. The stories had told of five score buried here, but Djaga could see now that there was one last sarcophagus standing apart from the rest—the hundred and first.

Djaga was suddenly fearful of approaching it. "What does it mean?"

"It means that her story was lost to the passage of time, nothing more. Now quit acting like a scared little grass maiden and help me open it." She motioned to the place beside her. "Unless you wish to weave baskets and paint gourds for the rest of your life."

Djaga moved to stand beside the last of the sarcophagi. *Their leader, surely.* Together, they pried the lid up. When they pushed it aside, the harsh scraping echoed eerily. It felt like an affront to the gods. Inside the sarcophagus, barely visible, were a pair of desiccated legs held loosely together with a cord woven from stalks of grass. Upon the toes were golden rings. Around the right ankle were three bands of gold.

"Those," Afua said, pointing to the anklets.

Djaga swallowed. "You're sure?"

As Afua reached in and slipped one of the anklets around the foot, the cord of grass crumbled as if it were made of ash. "Stop asking me that." She held the anklet up, admiring it, then took off the rope sandal on her right foot and slipped it on. When she noticed Djaga hadn't moved to do the same, she snapped her fingers. "Hurry up, you moon-eyed girl!"

Djaga took one deep breath. *I do this for you, Sjado.* She reached in and slipped the second anklet from around the frail foot but, unlike Afua, slipped it around her own ankle while hardly looking at it. That done, they quickly moved to the opposite side of the sarcophagus and shouldered the stone lid home. Djaga shivered as it boomed shut.

"Let's go," Djaga said. "The air is pressing down on me." She refused to run—the two-faced god would not be pleased if she did—but neither did she dawdle. Soon they had made it out and had done their best to close the crypt door. It was too heavy, though, and they had no leverage. They managed to scrape it only a little before they gave up and began heading back toward the village.

Only then did Djaga realize she felt no different. No different at all. The anklet did not make her feel closer to Sjado, as Afua had promised. It only filled her with shame.

In the fighting pits of Sharakhai, Djaga's battle with Talashem continued. In the tempest of her swings, her awareness of Afua was nearly, though not completely, lost. Why she'd come to Sharakhai, and why *now*, were mysteries Djaga had yet to solve, but of this much she could be sure: it was a tale that could only end in misery.

Talashem was no fool. He saw Djaga's preoccupation and knew enough to press the advantage. His shamshir spun, dealing blow after blow. Djaga was barely able to fend him off. When he followed a block with a furious charge that knocked her off balance and drove the spike at the center of his shield into her shoulder, the pain and the blood brought her back to this place, to the dirt, to the warrior before her, to the satisfying heft of the club in her hand.

For you, Sjado. All is for you.

After blocking Talashem's sword low, she spun

around his shield and the head of her spiked club into his back. His armor blunted the blow, but he reeled from the pain and backed away, trying to regain his center. But Djaga advanced too quickly. She ducked a hasty swipe of his sword, kicked his knee, causing him to buckle, and drove her club against the side of his shield when he raised it. She put the whole of her body, the whole of her years of rage, into that blow. The release felt sweet. The club landed so hard it dented the shield's edge and sent Talashem reeling.

That one small opening gave her all the time she needed. She raised the club and drove it against the top of his helm. The blow rang sharply against the metal, but beneath it was the satisfying sound of a meaty strike. Talashem collapsed, his body spasming several times before he came to a rest, arms splayed against the pit's dirt floor.

The crowd raised their hands to the desert sky, cheering as one. Djaga's breath came in great huffs, her rage still wrapped around her like a flaming cloak. She turned, examining the crowd, forgetting who or what she'd been looking for. The crowd thought it was for them, and their full-throated roar rose to new heights.

Then her purpose returned. Afua. She was looking for Afua.

But she was gone. Just as Djaga had been able to sense Afua's presence earlier, she sensed her absence now. Afua was no longer in or near the pits.

Djaga's eyes swung to gaze at Nadín. None of the worry she'd shown earlier had ebbed. She'd seen Djaga's frantic search for Afua for what it was, and was as worried for Djaga as she'd been before the bout had begun.

How can I explain it to you? Djaga thought.

She couldn't—she'd hidden too much from Nadín—so instead she turned and headed down the cold, darkened tunnel.

Afua came two days later. Djaga was working on Nadín's ship, *Yerinde's Needle*, repairing the sails as Nadín had taught her. It was calming work, sandships. Always something to do. Always something to take Djaga's mind away from Sjado's hunger, which some days felt as if it were gnawing at her from the inside. The feeling never truly left her, but simple, hard, physical labor, was one of the most effective remedies. As was fighting. The days after a bout were always the most peaceful for her, Sjado's appetite having been fed to some degree.

The harbor's kaleidoscope of sounds mingled with the hot breeze. The dull pounding of a hammer. The sad call of an amberlark hiding in the shade beneath a pier. Old Ibrahim telling a story, coins clinking as patrons tossed them onto the carpet he'd laid out for just that purpose. From the harbor's opposite side came the shrill voice of a woman hawking her wares. "Elixirs, my lords," she called to those walking by. "Elixirs made from the fabled dune drake, known across the desert for bringing a twinkle to your eye, a thing your lady love will thank you for." The western harbor was a ragtag assemblage, to be sure, but they were Djaga's adopted family as well. She'd accepted them early, and they, with Nadín's help, had accepted her in return. It was this as much as the work on the sandships that Djaga loved.

Finishing a line of stitches in the canvas, Djaga arched her back, working out the kinks. Nadín stood not far away on the deck, waving with a smile to someone along the quay. She looked beautiful standing there, as much a part of the ship as the lateen sails or the skimwood runners.

Nadín, catching Djaga's gaze, stared down at her. "And what do *you* find so interesting?"

"You."

Her stern look turned to a smile. "I am nothing."

"You are the brightness of the sun as it shines through the rain."

She looked as if she were going to brush the compliment aside, a thing she always did when Djaga showered her with praise, but the words seemed to die on her lips as she stared out to the end of the pier. Footsteps approached, thumping along the pier's heavy planks. Djaga knew without turning who it would be; she had the same feeling as she'd had in the pits.

As Djaga stood and turned, she was back in the grasslands, stealing the artifacts of the dead, ready to use them so that the gods might witness her. *And they had,* Djaga thought, a flash of dead bodies swimming before her eyes. She blinked and shook her head, focusing on the approaching woman once more.

The Afua now heading down the pier walked with a bit of a limp, and of course she appeared older than Djaga's memories—she was now on the lean side of thirty summers, just like Djaga—but otherwise she looked remarkably similar to the years they'd spent together in the grasslands, especially the smile on her face, the demon's glint in her eyes.

That was how her grandfather had always described her: *that little demon.* He'd been joking, of course—

the sort of thing a grandfather said to get a mother riled—but it had stuck. It was as much a part of Afua as her broad cheeks, her rounded chin.

"Good day to you, Djaga," Afua said in Kundhunese.

"What are you doing here?" Djaga replied.

"I've been in Sharakhai for some time." Afua looked over the ship with a pinched expression, as if she'd come to buy it but now found it wanting. "I've been meaning to seek you out."

"And only now found the courage?"

"Who is this, my sweet?" Nadín asked in Sharakhan.

Afua turned to face Nadín, but continued to speak to Djaga in their tribal language. "I'm surprised you haven't told your little pet about me. I'm sure you sensed me in the pits. Are you *embarrassed* of me, Djaga?"

Pet, Afua had called her, which meant she knew about the two of them. "You've been watching me...."

"In *Sharakhan*, if you please." Nadín took a step toward Afua with a look that could wither stone. She was not a tall woman, Nadín, but in that moment she looked every bit Afua's equal. "And tell her to stop staring at me with that smug smile of hers before I smash it off her face."

Djaga moved quickly to Nadín and took her hand, easing her away from Afua. "Forgive me. Afua is my cousin, raised in the same village as I. We haven't seen one another in some time. Afua, this is Nadín."

Though clearly annoyed, Nadín gave Afua a bow of her head. Afua returned the gesture crisply, almost coldly, then considered Djaga anew. "The news I have is for you alone," she said, thankfully in Sharakhan.

Djaga squeezed Nadín's hand. "I need but a moment."

Nadín was wary, and tight as a bowstring, but she trusted Djaga. After a pause in which she regained her composure, she nodded and went belowdecks as if there were more important things that needed tending to. Djaga motioned Afua to sit along the gunwales, but Afua jutted her chin toward the end of the pier. "Let's take to the sand."

Djaga shrugged and followed her. They took the ladder down and strode away from the ship, making for the center of the harbor's expanse. "Now what is it you want?"

"Want?" Afua laughed, a bark that rose above the wash of sounds around them. "I'm here to *help* you, cousin."

"Help me? My life was *ruined* because of you."

"If I recall it rightly, you were right by my side when we entered the barrow. You took the pry bar from my hands willingly!"

Djaga had never forgotten the shame of what she and Afua had done, but it hadn't felt so deep as this, not in a long time, not since coming to Sharakhai. Djaga stopped walking. "You've come to help, you say, but first you wish to rub my nose in my failures?"

Afua stopped and turned, the skirt of her purple dress flaring as she did so. "Forgive me." She took a deep breath and pinched the bridge of her nose. "It feels like yesterday. I'm sure it does for you as well. But I *have* come to help you. I've come to release you from the torture you've endured."

There was always a gnawing feeling within Djaga. With the rage she'd expended in the pits the other day, it was little more than a simmer, but when Afua had said these words, the feeling began to roil once more. "Release me from what?"

"Don't be thick. I know what's plagued you. You know the same of me. The two-faced god, Djaga. Sjado's rage lives inside me, Jonsu's peace ever out of reach. Can you say it isn't the same for you?"

Though it felt strange to admit it, Djaga felt exactly

the same. She'd never told anyone. Not the people of her village when they'd held her for trial. Not Osman, the owner of the pits. Not Nadín. Even here, standing before a woman who knew her tale, who knew her shame, Djaga couldn't say it aloud. It felt too much like blasphemy.

"What of it?" Djaga finally asked.

"You can be free of it. I've found a way!"

A storm threatened the horizon as Djaga and Afua jogged over the grasslands. Over the stand of low trees that marked the northern edge of their village, a twisting column of smoke rose into an overcast sky. The scent of wood smoke came to them, and roasting gazelle, one small portion of the feast that would be consumed when the rites of passage had been completed.

As they reached the dirt road and passed through the stone archway, people began waving to them from the doorways of their huts. "Be stout," old Elu called to them, her gray hair wild, her smile even wilder. "Be stout and you'll win the heart of the goddess."

Afua and Djaga shared a look. Afua smiled, but it

was forced. She'd said over and over that there was no harm in touching the artifacts of the fabled warriors—*that we would risk so much will prove our passion*—but even *she* must be having doubts by now.

Soon they'd arrived at the village center. Hundreds moved about, readying all for the ritual and the feast to follow. Tall wooden posts had been freshly painted in red and white and yellow. Hanging from each was a horsetail dyed indigo and blue. The wind played with them, made them flutter in alternating rhythms as the southern storm pressed closer. The mock battlefield—little more than a shallow depression—held a number of the other aspirants already. Djaga's uncle and brother were talking with one another at the edge, along with others from the temple.

"And there she is," her uncle said, arms spread wide. They hugged. His tall headdress, made of bright beads and painted quills, rustled and clicked as he moved. He introduced her to others from nearby villages, who had come to witness her in her attempt to join the temple of the two-faced god. Her brother brought her fermented horse milk and bade her drink it quickly. It would make her shine more brightly to the gods, he said. She took it, not because she believe him, but because she thought it might quell her nerves.

Her ankle burned from the weight of the gold wrapped around it. She and Afua had stopped on the run back home and covered them with mud, but to Djaga it looked like a child had done it. How could they not see what it truly was? How could they not point and name them blasphemers?

Djaga nearly went to tell her uncle to confess it all, but just then Afua strode up to her and gripped her by the elbow, holding her in place. "Will you calm yourself?"

"I want to take it *off*, Afua. The shame of it burns my skin."

"We did it for a reason. Now find your nerve, girl. Sjado rewards the *bold*."

Time and again, the old tales spoke of Sjado winning at any cost—against mighty Hiwe, against swift Pemaru, against even Onondu, using his own tricks against him—before the aspect of the warrior faded and peaceful Jonsu rose to prominence once more.

"It still feels shameful."

Afua's face grew angry. She gripped Djaga's arm to the point of pain. "Bury your shame, girl, and find your heart. You'll not deny me this day." She softened a moment later, and nodded to Djaga's uncle. "This is as much for him as it is for you. You know as well as I how his heart will swell with pride when the mark of the warrior is cut into your skin."

She watched her uncle, who had become like a father to her and Idé after their true father had died five years earlier in their tribe's ceaseless border skirmishes with the neighboring Halawari. Just then he was smiling as the King of a nearby tribe told a story, motioning to his daughter, who had been a member of Sjado's temple for years now. Djaga could tell her uncle was smiling not for the King, who was a blowhard if Djaga had ever heard one, but for how proud he would be should Djaga be accepted as well.

"I just want this day to be done."

"It will all be over soon." Afua smiled. "In the flit of a hummingbird's wings."

The next hour passed like a dream. Greeting the dozens who'd traveled from leagues all around. Taking the sacrament of goat's blood. Being painted with yellow clay by the high priestess herself, a woman with green eyes that seemed to pierce Djaga's heart.

Soon Djaga, Afua, and five others were ready to take their final test. Rattling circlets were tied around their wrists and ankles. They were granted spears and tall, wickerwork shields. They were stood in a tight circle in the center of the ritual's arena. And then seven full initiates of Sjado's temple were arrayed around them with spears and shields of their own.

The task was simple: draw blood before submitting or being forced to withdraw. Not so easy considering how well the initiates to Sjado's temple were trained, but something that young aspirants were often able to do on their first or second ritual day. But Afua hadn't been convinced it would be enough. She'd wanted to impress. So had Djaga. But now all she could think about was the stolen anklet and how it weighed on her.

"Through war we find peace," the high priestess was saying.

"Through war we find peace," Djaga and the others intoned.

And then the high priestess swung a whip over her head and sent it to cracking over the aspirant's heads. Immediately, the initiates closed in. Djaga lowered in her stance, ready to defend herself, but the woman across from her was so swift she got in a strike against Djaga's shin before Djaga was even set. Djaga winced and backed away, lowering her shield. But when she did that her opponent thrust the spear lightning quick and scored another strike against her leading shoulder.

Djaga tried to counterattack, but her thrust was met by the orange shield. Her heart pounded in her chest. The sounds around her—the battle cries of the warriors, the shouts of the crowd, the screaming of the children—all became a wash, a numbing rattle akin to the monsoons of the wet season as rain drove hard against the grasses. That was when Djaga first felt it. A presence. Like the one she'd felt as a child when she went out alone to the grasslands at night. It was an indescribable fear, surely the presence of Odokōn, the god of death who came for all. Djaga had run back to the village to her home. She'd buried her face in her mother's breast and cried, and her mother had consoled her until she'd fallen asleep at last.

There would be no running now, and Odokōn had already come for her mother. This was a thing undeniable. A demand from Sjado herself for Djaga to fulfill her desires. *Battle leads to salvation. War is how we survive.* Djaga felt the goddess move within her. Felt her take up her shield, felt her heft her spear. Sjado moved, sinuous as a mamba, spear darting, sinking deep into flesh.

She heard grunts of pain, heard shouts of surprise. She became the kingfisher, flitting between dull thrusts of weapons held in deadened hands. She became the acacia, stout against the blows brought against her. She became the midnight finch, drinking the blood of her enemies. One fell, a spear cutting her throat. Another dropped holding her stomach where the spear had pierced her through. Others came. Tried to swarm her. But she was the wind. She was the storm. She was the strike of lightning and the bellow of thunder.

One by one, all that stood against her fell to the ground, until none remained in the arena but the dead. She held her spear to the sky and released the almighty rage that still burned in her veins. She shouted for any to come near. But none would. They'd seen the goddess in her, and they feared.

She nearly went to them, nearly charged to take more with her spear. Among them, however, she spied a woman, staring at her from just outside the circle, her spear, still to hand, pointing at Djaga as if she feared she would be the next victim. It was Afua.

The storm winds blew, tossing the horsetails while all else was still.

You left the arena.

The wind blew, cool against her burning skin.

You left, and this was all your idea.

The wind blew, and the rain began to fall.

I 've found a way!

The words hung between Afua and Djaga like a mirage. This was trickery, Djaga knew, nothing more. She already knew the way to release, and it was through atonement, through giving Sjado what she wanted. One day the two-faced god would judge her worthy of becoming her own woman once more. Not before. And yet the possibility of release, of Afua knowing some secret Djaga had overlooked, was so tantalizing that Djaga found herself saying, "How?"

"Do you see the man standing at the end of that pier?"

Djaga turned to look. On the pier stood a stout Malasani man. His hair was cut straight over his brow, an echo of sorts to his simple black tunic. He had a rough-and-tumble look about him—an ever-hungry wolf, sated for the moment. She'd never met the man but she recognized him immediately. She'd seen him twice, in the killing pits.

"That's Hathahn," Djaga said, already starting to understand what Afua wanted of her.

"Very good."

"You wish me to fight him. In the killing pits."

Afua bowed her head, the sly nod of a merchant toward a particularly wealthy patron. "Your final bout flies ever nearer, does it not?"

"I refuse to kill, Afua. You've been here in Sharakhai long enough. You must know that by now."

"Yes, I've been watching you. I've asked around the pits as well. But I know the girl you *were*." Afua's face turned sour. "You hope to appease *Sjado* by toying with your food and never eating it? You should have known even before your first bout, but surely you know it by now—it will *never* work, Djaga. Sjado demands her due."

"You've found your own peace, then?"

Afua smiled, an expression as sad as a thunderstorm over the grasslands. "I've done my killing. But I cannot be free until you are. We are bound. How could it be any other way?"

It made sense. They had entered the arena together. Afua might have left before it was done, but what would that mean to the two-faced god? Sjado would have punished her as well, and why not bind them together like Sjado was bound to Jonsu?

"Is that it, then? You wish to find release if I kill Hathahn and appease Sjado?"

"You are a warrior, Djaga, a thing you deny despite playing at war in the pits. Sjado's wrath will be quenched only when you kill, not before. When that is done, I will lead us both to Jonsu's peace."

Djaga looked to where the brute, Hathahn, stood at the end of the pier. He was watching them as if he were curious, nothing more, though this had as much to do with him as it did Djaga and Afua. "Just like that? He'll lie down and let me kill him?"

"Of course not. He's long heard of you, and when I told him I might convince you to join him in the killing pits for your final bout, he quickly agreed. To his own god would go the glory."

Djaga crossed her arms, turning away from the wind and the biting sand for a moment until it had died down. "I took a vow."

Afua's face screwed up in anger. "Wake up, girl! Who do you think was it that took those lives? Was it you? Me? No, it was Sjado herself. She was angry with us, true, but she was showing us her very nature. I have been haunted by her and Jonsu ever since. Neither of us will find peace until we atone for our sins."

"I took a vow."

Afua stared at her for a time, but then she huffed like one of the desert's bone crushers. "You would deny yourself *peace*?"

"I haven't seen you in a dozen years. After all this time, after abandoning me in Kundhun, after leaving me to wonder what had happened to you, you darken my doorway reciting honeyed tales of how *I* might be freed from the chains of the gods, and you would have me believe that it's for *my* benefit?"

Afua raised her hands to the sky, shook them as if she were calling for rain. "I want to set things *right*, Djaga! I want to right at least *one* of the wrongs I've committed." When Djaga continued to stare coldly, a crack formed in Afua's composed face. "Do I not deserve *some* peace in this life?"

"I won't do it."

"You *must*."

"You may not believe that vows have meaning, Afua, but I do." She began heading back toward Nadín's ship, the supple sand grasping at the soles of her boots. "Go. Return to Hathahn and tell him you'll need to find another, for I'll not fight him, no matter how much you plead."

Nadín stood at the ship's small stove, stirring a pot of soup. "So she left you there to face the tribunal alone?"

It was well past sundown, but it had taken a long

while to explain it all to Nadín. Djaga had never told her the truth. Not all of it anyway. When she'd learned more, she'd wanted the rest, and Djaga had finally relented. It was the lowest moment of Djaga's life, a thing she was shamed to even speak of, but it she were going to start a new life with Nadín, she needed to share it or she'd be living a lie.

"Yes, she left me, though I don't blame her for it. Not anymore. The tribunal would have ordered her death. I'm sure of it."

"Maybe she *deserved* to die."

Djaga shrugged. "I don't decide who lives and who dies."

Nadín frowned at that, but said nothing in return. After ripping two hunks of bread so dark it was nearly black and dropping it into the waiting bowls, she turned and leaned against the hull. Her arms were crossed and she was giving Djaga that stare or hers, the one that said she wouldn't be satisfied until she knew everything. "Why didn't they kill you?"

"They were scared." Djaga could still remember it, the look of fear in their eyes as they stared at her, blood coating her spear, dead bodies all around. "Every single one of them."

"Scared you would fight them?"

"The *goddess* was in me, Nadín. They'd seen it, and they were afraid she'd come for everyone else. They didn't know yet what Afua and I had done, and even after I'd confessed they still wondered at Sjado's intentions. No one had witnessed her like that in generations. Kill me, and they risked Sjado's wrath."

Nadín ladled soup into bowls, dousing the hunks of day-old bread, then topped it with a sprinkling of chopped parsley. She set one before Djaga, then took the chair across from her at the small galley table. She blew on the soup, then slurped a spoonful noisily.

This is what I want, Djaga thought. *Me and Nadín on a ship, far away from the violence of Osman's pits.*

In the days ahead, she planned to sail with Nadín and trade with the people of her tribe far to the west of Sharakhai. They'd sail to other tribes and trade with them as well. Then they'd return to Sharakhai and sell the goods and use a portion of the proceeds buy more to fill their hold, enough for another voyage out to the baking sands. It would be a simple life, but a life Djaga would treasure. If only she could enjoy it. Nadín had been after her for months to leave the pits once and for all.

Djaga had scoffed at first. "I know nothing else," she'd told Nadín one night as they lay in bed.

"I'll teach you," Nadín had said, leaning in to kiss her.

"I'm an old lion, with teeth and claws and little else."

"Are you saying you *can't* learn"—she ran her fingers along the riddle of scars that marked Djaga's arm—"or that you don't wish to?"

Djaga grabbed a fistful of Nadín's hair, pulled her near, and kissed her soft lips more deeply than Nadín had done a moment ago. "I'm saying I am a beast trapped in a Kundhuni's skin. I'm saying no amount of hoping will change that."

"It will only take *time*, my sweet."

Time, Djaga thought. It sounded so reasonable. More and more, though, as the day of her retirement approached, she worried it was only a foolish wish and nothing more. She hadn't been able to find the peace she'd hoped would come with the knowledge that she would soon leave the pits. And now she worried that it would *never* come. Already the itch to fight was on her. Already it was making her want to push Nadín away. Soon it would become a need, and then, if it wasn't quenched in some way, the goddess would come to occupy her form as she had in Kundhun.

I must find a way. I will die before I let anything

happen to Nadín.

"You're looking at me like that again."

"Like what?"

"Like you're lost."

I am lost. In a wasteland of my god's own making.

Nadín motioned to Djaga's bowl. "Eat."

Djaga picked up the spoon and used its edge to hack off a spoonful of bread. It was good, the two together, the silky, saffron-laced broth with the earthy bread.

"You never saw Afua again?" Nadín asked.

"Not until today."

"The way she strutted up to my ship," Nadín said under her breath, "acting as if she's some queen from the grasslands."

As if her words had summoned it, there came the sound of footsteps on the pier outside their ship. But the tread was heavy, the stride long. "Djaga Akoyo?"

Djaga didn't recognize the man's voice. It was deep, resonant. "Who's come?"

The reply came in a thick Malasani accent. "It is Hathahn. I've come to speak to you and your woman."

Nadín frowned, her eyes flitting between the hatch door and Djaga. *What does he want?* she mouthed to Djaga.

Djaga could only shrug. She had no idea. When Djaga raised her eyebrows, asking Nadín for her permission for Hathahn to board her ship, Nadín nodded, though none of her nervousness subsided.

"Come," Djaga said.

In a moment, Hathahn's ample backside was taking the ladder down into the hold. He wore a striped tunic of white and red. He had thick bracelets of beaten steel on his well-muscled arms and a torc of twisted gold around his neck, a thing that did more to accentuate the corded muscles along his shoulders than the wide neck of his tunic did.

Nadín's reaction to Hathahn's sudden arrival was anything but pleased, but she still stood and motioned to the stove. "Would you like some soup?"

Hathahn raised his hands, forestalling her. "I cannot stay long, thank you. I've only come to speak to Djaga for a moment, and you as well, if you'd care to hear my tale."

"Very well," Nadín said, and before Djaga could say anything against her, she sat and motioned Hathahn to the nearby bench that doubled as their bed when pulled out and laid flat. Djaga wouldn't have denied her anyway, for she had no doubt this was something Nadín would need a voice in.

"Where do I begin?" Hathahn said, his legs spread wide, his hands on his knees. Gods, the man was huge. He made the galley look tiny by his mere presence. He waved one of his meaty platters-for-hands toward Djaga. "My Afua came to you today. She told you a tale that would appeal to your sense of, shall we say, self-preservation."

"Self-preservation!" Nadín, her soup forgotten, crossed her arms over her chest. "You call fighting a man like you *self-preservation*?"

Hathahn nodded. "We preserve ourselves in this life, and we preserve ourselves for the next, yes? We must think not only of our bodies, but our very *souls*. Unless I'm sadly mistaken"—he fixed his steely gaze on Djaga—"this is a thing that concerns you. Does it not?"

Djaga was beginning to get annoyed with her life being interrupted. "Get on with it."

The smile on Hathahn's broad face was a knowing one. "We worry about many things. Our health. Our livelihood." He turned his gaze on Nadín. "Our ability to provide for our loved ones." He paused then, leaning back, the wooden bench creaking beneath his weight. "You know that I'm a slave, yes?"

"I know," Djaga said.

He shrugged. "Your look shows pity, but in truth

I've had a fine life. I was raised to fight. I enjoyed it. I grew good at it." He smiled and leaned forward, eyeing Djaga with a jackal grin. "Very good at it." He shrugged again. "But the teeth of all dogs grow blunt. Our bite becomes less sharp. You must know."

Djaga stared, hating this reminder of all she was.

"My master hails from Malasan," Hathahn went on. "I have four wives there. I have twelve children. It's been two years since I've seen them, and I have no illusions that I'll ever see them alive again in this life. I live to fight. And now that I've risen as high as I can, I will fight until I am killed. Why? Because I care only for two things. That my family will prosper and grow, and that I will stand on the shore of the river, celebrated by our gods as my family crosses over to meet me, one by one. My master will not only provide for them, he will see to their welfare, for in me they have a champion of Malasan. A warrior like Shonokh incarnate."

"I grow tired of your tale, Hathahn."

"You do?" He laughed, a deep rumble that filled that confined space. "Then you'll bore yourself to tears when your days in the pits are done. I tell you these things so that you will know my intent. I want this to be—how do they say it in Kundhun?—clear as the spring rains." He eyed her up and down, a feral look in his dark eyes. "I will not lie down for you, Djaga Akoyo. I will not lie down so that Afua can give you this gift, so that you may be released from your foolishness. I would not lie down if your bitch goddess, Sjado, were she to stand before me now. Be it you or a Blade Maiden or a King of Sharakhai, I will kill the dog who stands against me in the pits or I will die fighting to my last breath. When I depart these shores, I will go to the farther fields with my sword in hand and my head held high."

"Why are you telling her this?" Nadín asked, her face aghast.

Hathahn didn't look at her. His eyes were only for Djaga. "I tell you this so that you will know. With you and I in the pit? It will be a fight that will summon the eyes of all the gods. Malasan, the Great Shangazi, even the gods of the lazy hills of Kundhun." He stood, hunkered over in the low space, then poked her in the chest, and tried to do so again until Djaga slapped his hand away and stood herself. "Were you to fight me, your god will listen. And if she doesn't?" He spat wetly onto the floorboards between them. "Then she never will. That is the promise a fight with me will bring."

He swung his gaze to Nadín, then back to Djaga. He looked coiled, ready to spring. Djaga readied herself, but then Hathahn relaxed. He licked his lips and smiled, then turned and strode toward the stairs. "Or fight another sad dog, and see then how your life with your soft tribeswoman turns out."

He was soon gone. The heavy tread of his steps on the pier slowly faded, but the stink of his musk lingered. Djaga found herself breathing hard, her hands shaking. Worst of all, though, was the fact that the hunger in her had exploded like a dawning sun inside her. It took all her effort to sit, to pick up her spoon, to spoon the now-tasteless soup into her mouth.

Nadín said nothing, but she knew everything Djaga was feeling. Djaga could tell by her cold silence.

L ate that night, Nadín lay by Djaga's side in the ship's lone bunk. Nadín's skin was warm against hers. They way she and Nadín had made love after, in such a mechanical way, had made her feel worse than when Hathahn had left. Afua and her machinations had ruined that as well.

Nadín raked her fingers over Djaga's short hair. It was normally a thing that felt so good. Tonight it grated. She let Nadín do it anyway. She knew it was

Hathahn's doing. She'd already felt out of sorts before he'd come to the ship, but it had only been magnified by the strange way he'd spoken to her, as if he could browbeat her into fighting him.

Say what you will, she could hear Afua saying. *He was only telling you the truth.*

Somewhere out in the desert, the grunts of a black laugher were followed by the yip of a jackal. Nadín stilled her movements, then pulled Djaga's jaw toward her until they were eye-to-eye in the moonlight spilling through the nearby porthole. "Why did you never tell me all of this?"

Djaga shrugged. "How could I?"

Nadín smiled a knowing smile. "One word at a time."

"Each describing my shame more fully."

Nadín shook her head. "There's no shame in the truth. You were only trying to please your goddess. And there's no shame in asking for help, either."

A tear slipped from the corner of Djaga's eye, a tear which Nadín wiped away. "I don't know what to do, my love. I keep asking myself how I can please her. She's insatiable. I feel her, always, gnawing at me from the inside. It's already growing worse. She wants more and more." She went on before Nadín could reply. "I know you think it will pass in time. And there's a part of me that hopes it's true, but I worry she will never let me go for what I've done. I worry my debt will never be paid. Not until I pass beyond these shores."

Nadín was quiet for a long while. She licked her lips before speaking. "Could there be truth to it?"

Djaga knew exactly what she meant. "Of course there could."

"But there's no way to know."

"No."

Nadín used her fingers to rub away the tear in Djaga's other eye. "Will Osman find a better fighter than Hathahn?"

Djaga weighed her words carefully before speaking. She thought she knew where Nadín was headed, but she didn't want to influence her. "One never knows. But Hathahn is as vicious a fighter as Sharakhai has seen in decades. Those that have been watching the pit fights for generations all say it is so."

"Then fight him," Nadín said. "If you don't, and Sjado continues to haunt you, you'll always wonder if he might have freed you. And in him you can be freed of your guilt. He *wants* to die, Djaga. It's like the goddess herself set this task before you. I don't wish you to fight, but you've one last fight ahead, so do this. Fight him. Send him to meet his god. Deliver his pride to his family." She leaned in and kissed Djaga, her lips warm and supple. "Free yourself."

Freedom. The very word felt foreign. She'd been running from her own past, her own goddess, for years, but it had gotten her nowhere. *No,* she thought, *it brought me to Nadín.* And yet it felt like a mirage. She'd been telling herself for years that when she found someone, she could leave the pits behind. Surely the goddess wouldn't keep hold of her forever. But now it seemed she would. Her love for Nadín would not last if the goddess continued to gnaw at her day and night. Or at the very least, Nadín's love for her would not last. It would whither away like a rose cut and left beneath the desert sun.

Afua wouldn't have come all this way to betray Djaga again. She had a debt to pay, and she was paying it. High time she started to take responsibility for what had happened.

This time, she was the one to lean in and offer a kiss. When she pulled away, she stared into Nadín's beautiful brown eyes. "I'll do it."

The crowd in the central pit was as large as Djaga had ever seen. Thousands were packed so tightly a man could hardly raise his arms to cheer. But cheer they did. The sound of it was like a wall of sound pressing in on her and Hathahn, who paced across the dirt floor opposite her, staring at the crowd and waving his hand as if he were the savior of Sharakhai.

Osman's pits were not killing pits. Osman had never had a taste for it—*it wastes lives needlessly*, he'd told her more than once—but all knew that this match would be to the death. It had drawn the rich from far and wide. The merchant class. Those born to money. People from a dozen nearby caravanserais had traveled to Sharakhai merely to attend. The highborn of Sharakhai stood in the four boxes set aside for lords and ladies of such means. None of the Kings had been announce by Pelam, but Djaga wouldn't be surprised if one of them had come in disguise.

Of all the people in the pit, Djaga watched only for two: Nadín and Afua, neither of whom were in attendance. She knew Nadín hadn't come, for Djaga had set aside a seat for her to the right of Osman's box. And though Djaga searched for her in the avalanche of faces around her, she knew Afua was gone as well—she would have felt her presence otherwise.

She had little time to wonder at Afua's absence, however, for Pelam was already introducing her. Even five paces away she could barely hear him as he called, "The Lion of Kundhun!" When he waved, the ground beneath her shook from the stomping, from the unified, undignified roar of the crowd. It went on a long while, and Djaga needed every bit of it. As hungry as she'd been for battle in the days leading up to this bout, she was confused now. Worried. But she knew she would need Sjado if she was to have any chance of defeating Hathahn.

Like a virtuoso actor who knew how to draw just the right notes of emotion from his audience, Pelam waited until the din had diminished. Only then did he wave to Hathahn and introduce him as the Butcher of Malasan, a title he'd earned time and time again in the pits. Again the crowd's frenzy built on itself. In all her time in the pits, Djaga had never seen the like, but she was beginning to master her emotions at last.

She paced the pit floor, swinging her arms in circles, flexing her muscles to loosen them. The voice of the crowd deadened in her ears. They became little more than a part of the pit, akin to the walls, akin to the vault of the open sky above them. Her attention was now for Hathahn and Hathahn alone. He was not merely calm. He was like a statue, standing tall, his broad face utterly serene. Only his eyes moved as Djaga paced the pit floor. He hardly seemed to be breathing.

It was likely a way to put her off balance, but if that was so, it wouldn't work. Djaga could feel the goddess once more. *I ask not for your favor, Sjado. I ask not for your favor. I only give what you require...*

They were words she'd spoken thousands of times. The only way the two-faced god had ever acknowledged them was through the rage that built within Djaga. Sjado might consider that answer enough, and Djaga had never presumed to ask for more, but today was different. She needed more. She deserved it after this long in the service of the two-faced god.

She stopped her pacing and faced Hathahn. "This day," she shouted, her words lost in the terrible din like smoke in a sandstorm, "I would know the truth!"

This was her last hope. She would either die or she would kill Hathahn. And if killing him didn't work, she would know that her efforts in the years since that terrible day in her village had been in vain. She would know as well that the curse laid upon her since she'd slain her friends and family in Kundhun was permanent.

The crowd hushed as the weapons were brought

out by three pit boys. Hathahn chose a pair of beaten
battle axes. Djaga took two khopeshes, the sharply
curved swords of the grasslands. Pelam now stood
between them, his small brass gong in hand, mallet raised high. In an instant, the noise of the crowd
hushed. The moment Pelam struck the gong, Djaga
charged forth, releasing a battle cry as she moved to
meet Hathahn in battle.

Hathahn met her onslaught with apparent ease.
He blocked her swings, the sound of her blades on
the metal haft a ringing call to the heavens. Twice in
that early flurry he tried to hook a khopesh with the
head of an axe and rip it from her grasp, but she was
ready for it and used the momentary opening to snap
a kick into his stomach.

By Sjado's black breath, he was *solid*. He was also as
smooth a fighter as Djaga had ever come across. There
were no wasted movements as he blocked and retreated,
as he swung his axes in tight arcs before him. He was
playing a long game, hoping to let Djaga wear herself
out. But she was well used to such things. The power
of Sjado urged her on, to draw blood, but she bottled
the desire, used it instead to build her own anger.

Slowly, as sweat glistened upon their skin, as their
weapons bit and took small nicks from their armor,

her rage built like the glow of forge-kissed steel. She burned from it, red then orange then yellow then white. With each blow she released a powerful shout. They became more ragged, then slid into a roar as all her frustration from her time since leaving the grasslands for the desert—the shame over what she'd done to her own people, her feelings of abandonment by Afua—came out in one long outpouring, an offering for her god that she might have mercy.

Hathahn was methodical in his defense, axes pinwheeling to block Djaga's swords, helm or greaves or pauldrons taking the blows when Djaga was too quick. But then he did something that showed why he'd won so many matches in the killing pits. He waited for the perfect moment, driving through her defenses like a battering ram. Djaga retreated, scoring a deep cut into the meat of Hathahn's thigh, but he was on the move now, dropping an axe and grabbing her wrist as he came. He bulled forward, sending her crashing into the wall behind her. He drove his helm onto the crown of her head.

Hathahn stood in sharp contrast to Djaga. His eyes were serene. His breath smelled like freshly turned clay. He was a pinnacle of stone rising above the sand dunes, calm in the face of the storm.

"Come, you goat fucker," Djaga said. "It's time to *fight*." She dropped the sword in her free hand and sent two quick uppercuts into his jaw. Again it felt wrong, as if he were not flesh and bone, but something *else*. "Are you there, Hathahn?"

His only response was to stare with those deadened eyes and to twist her wrist. She immediately pushed away from the wall with all her might. When he tried to press his weight against her, she crouched low, grabbed one tree trunk of a thigh with her free arm, and lifted with all her might.

She knew immediately something was wrong. She'd lifted men his size before, but Hathahn was much heavier. And his skin was *hot*. As she powered him backward, he swiped at her with his axe, she felt the weapon bite, felt the burn spread near the base of her spine, but there was nothing for it now.

She drove him down to the ground, then rolled over him, twisting her arm free in one violent motion. He grabbed for her. She leaned away. He swiped for her ankles with his axe, but she was ready for it. She kicked the weapon's haft, halting it, then grabbed his wrist and dropped, snaking her legs around his arm. She leaned back, applying as much leverage to her lock on his arm as she could, wrenching it over and over until she heard a crack like the snapping of stone.

He'd held onto the axe the entire time, but when his arm broke, he'd released it. She took it up in one hand as she straddled his waist, then lifted it high in the air. She swung it down with all her might, sure Hathahn would try to stop her. But he didn't, and the head of the axe came down onto his helm, sundering it and his skull beneath. Blood leaked from the wound. It smelled acrid, though. Sulfurous. And his eyes. Jonsu's grace, they stared through her as if he were lying on a field of daisies staring at the deep blue sky.

As a long, guttural sigh escaped him, Djaga stood.

Chest heaving, she turned, ignoring the eruption of the crowd as they cheered for her. She looked desperately for Nadín, already knowing she wouldn't find her. A feeling of cold invaded her. Nadín was missing. Afua was gone. And now this—she stared down at the body lying at her feet—this *thing* that was not Hathahn. Had the tales of Malasan not spoken of golems created to mimic those whose blood had been taken? Surely this was one of those, make to look like Hathahn.

The door to the pit's subterranean tunnels had been slid open. Pelam was walking toward her, ready to raise her hand to the crowd, but she sprinted past him. She ran down the cold tunnel, through the labyrinth, and out the rearmost exit. Breath ragged, she willed her burning legs to keep pumping as she pounded her way toward the western harbor.

When Djaga reached the quayside, old Ibrahim the storyteller was there. For some reason he was walking toward her. "Best you come with me," he said as she came near.

"What's happened?"

He took her by the arm and led her toward an alley.

"Where are you—" Djaga stopped, for ahead there was a crowd gathered. A body was being lifted onto a cart. Blood coated the broken stones of the street. She rushed forward and saw what she already knew. She'd known from the moment she'd sprinted from the pit.

Those gathered tight around Nadín were from the harbor. The stevedores. The shipwrights. The merchants. The people Nadín had known all her life and whom Djaga had come to know through her. They stared at her, ashen-faced. Djaga moved to the cart's side and, by the grace of the gods, found Nadín breathing shallowly, staring up at the sky not so differently than Hathahn's dead form had done only minutes before. The way her hands were laid tenderly over her stomach—as if she'd simply eaten too much—was so incongruous with the bloody reality laid out on the bed of the cart that Djaga nearly retched.

She brushed the hair from Nadín's eyes. Leaned down and kissed her forehead. "Tell me what happened, my love."

Nadín blinked, her eyes distant. With effort, as if she were pulling her gaze away from the farther fields, she turned to stare into Djaga's eyes. "Hathahn."

The cart lurched into motion, the mule and the driver leading them toward the medicum. "What of him?" Djaga asked, moving to keep pace. Nadín swallowed. Licked her lips. Djaga took her hand and shook it. "Nadín, what of him?"

Nadín lifted one hand and stared at the blood, a deathbed smile distorting her features as if she still couldn't believe what had happened. "I've been stabbed."

A blade of ice slipped into Djaga's heart. "Nadín, quickly now!" She cradled Nadín's neck and shook her gently lest she slip back into unconsciousness. "Tell me what *happened*."

The look of confusion on Nadín's face was profound, as if with the answer to this question she could die in peace. "I was getting ready to leave for the pits when a messenger girl came. She said there was someone I'd be interested in seeing on the *Condor's Wake*. I told her I didn't care." She squeezed Djaga's fingers. "I told her I needed to go see you, but she said you were being fooled, that you were in danger, so of course I went. I saw five men preparing her to sail. I watched them for a time, but saw nothing strange. I was ready to leave when I heard his voice."

"Hathahn's?"

As the cart trundled around a corner and onto a wider thoroughfare, Nadín nodded. On even ground now, they began moving faster. "I dropped to the sand and moved to the rear of the ship. I saw him inside the rear cabin, talking to a man." She rolled her head back and forth. The pinch of her eyes wrung tears from them. "They saw me. They shouted for me to stop, but I ran. I ran across the whole of the harbor and then up to the quay. I was ready to make my way toward the pits, toward you, my love, when something flashed to my right." She lifted one shaking hand, coated in red. "And then this."

"Who?" Djaga asked, somehow already sure of the answer. "Who did this to you?"

Nadín shrugged, but winced immediately and fell

still, her breath coming in short gasps filled with soft, pitiful moans. "I remember the pain. I remember falling to the cobbles. I saw the hem of a thawb, but that was all, and then they were gone."

"Was it Afua?"

Nadín took a long time to respond to this. She looked as though she were debating. "I have no love for your cousin, but I cannot say."

They reached the front steps of the medicum, where a stretcher and two attendants were already waiting. As Nadín was being lifted down to the stretcher, Osman and three dirt dogs from the pits came running up from the direction of the harbor. They were all breathless.

"What's happened?" Osman said, his black brows pinched as he stared down at Nadín.

Djaga's fingers flexed. Her lips drew back as her lungs forced hot air through bared teeth. She'd never felt so out of control, not since Sjado had granted Djaga that first, cold kiss. She paced along the amber paving stones, staring at the buildings opposite the medicum. She wanted to tear them down. She wanted to tear the whole city down.

Osman took one step closer, reaching a hand out but stopping short of touching her. "Djaga, what's happened, girl?"

She stopped, glared at Osman. "A betrayal."

Osman glanced back at the dirt dogs, fighters from the pits that Djaga knew were very good. "You need help?"

Djaga hardly had to think about it. "Yes." But she couldn't do this alone. "Come," she said, and then they were off, running back toward the harbor.

Yerinde's Needle, Nadín's sleek, two-masted ketch, wasn't much for the eyes, but her skis were true and her sails were full. When she was like this, the wind to their backs and the dunes tight, she was swift as an amberlark. And she wasn't laden like the *Condor's Wake* was. The *Wake* was a dhow. It was larger. It had more men, and likely enough supplies for weeks of sailing, where the *Needle* was as light as they could make it.

They'd returned to the western harbor after leaving Nadín at the medicum. They'd searched for the ship Nadín had described, and found soon enough that it had left shortly before they'd arrived. They'd readied the ship as quickly as they could, the people of the harbor helping to tow the ship back, to get her moving as fast as they could.

They'd exited the harbor and sailed north, then eastward around the tip of Sharakhai. They spotted the *Condor* shortly after.

Steadily the *Needle* crept closer, the sand a bare whisper beneath the runners. Nightfall neared, and they came close enough that the crew on the other ship began firing arrows. At first it was merely to warn them away, but when it became clear they wouldn't be deterred, they started targeting Djaga at the wheel and the others about the ship. Osman set up some makeshift shields using the hatch cover and the table from the cabin belowdecks. It worked, and soon Hathahn's crew abandoned the tactic and from their hold brought up clay pots the size of oranges with black wicks sticking out from one end. They lit them afire and began launching them at the *Needle*.

The first struck the ship's port-side hull. The hull burst into flames, though thankfully most of it splashed downward onto the sand. The second hit the foredeck. Osman ran forward with dousing sand, one of the dirt dogs shielding him with the table to protect him from the renewed onslaught of arrows.

The *Needle* was running alongside the *Condor* now. Djaga called to the other pit fighter, Kaliban, "Take the wheel. Be ready to brake her."

"What are you going to do?" he asked as he stepped over.

Djaga eyed the other ship, where the bulky form of Hathahn had finally come up from the hold. "I'm going to take that rotting ship down."

As the crew of the dhow lit another flame pot, Djaga stepped over to the starboard gunwale. She took her long fighting knife from its sheath along her leg and bit down on it with her teeth. Grabbing the mainsail's halyard tight in her right hand. She crouched, and then, in one swift, furious motion, she pulled the belaying pin.

She leapt as the lanyard pulled with enough force to lift her from the deck. The wind in the mainsail, and the weight of the sail and its boom, drew her toward the top of the mainmast. She used her legs to run along it, guiding herself so that she'd be launched in the proper direction.

When she reached the top, the lanyard whipped her up and over the mast. She flew through the air as a fresh fire pot crashed below and spread its fire amidships. As she flew toward the dhow's triangular mainsail, she retrieved her knife from her teeth, gripped it tightly in both hands. The knife's tip met the sail's canvas, puncturing it with a sound like the beat of a drum.

Down she went toward the foot of the sail, her knife sizzling as it sliced the thick cloth neatly in two.

Hathahn charged across the deck to meet her, but when she reached the boom, she leapt backward, flipping high over him to land on the deck near the pilot's wheel. Her knife she drove deep into the pilot's neck. After snapping a kick into his chest to knock him aside, she spun the wheel, turning it over and over. It fought her the more the ship turned, but she kept going, muscles straining, until she'd turned it as far as it could go.

The ship heeled toward the starboard side as it turned sharply to port. The rudder, the central, rear ski, was now almost perfectly at odds with the line the ship had been moving in. It dragged, throwing Djaga forward against the wheel so hard she lost her grip on her knife. It went clattering forward across the deck, tossing sunlight as it went. The crew, who'd been rushing toward her, were thrown as well. They grabbed for the rigging to steady themselves, but several fell hard to the deck. They slid scrabbling toward the fore of the ship. Not Hathahn, though. He'd grabbed tight to the rigging. And now he came pounding forward, sending a powerful jab across Djaga's jaw, an uppercut that glanced across her skull, then a kick that sent her reeling.

She flailed for purchase, but so close to the stern there was nothing. The gunwale clipped her thighs as she flew backward over the deck's edge. She crashed onto the sand, and it knocked the breath from her.

She slid and rolled. The sand scraped roughly over her skin. Hathahn dropped from the ship moments before the prow of the *Needle* crashed into it with a sound like thunder. The sails of both ships shuddered as they came to rest at last.

Hathahn approached Djaga, scimitar in one hand, a fighting knife in the other. "Couldn't leave it alone, could you?"

Djaga stood.

"You could have let us leave. Live out your life in peace as the greatest warrior the pits had ever seen."

Djaga ignored him, undoing her leather belt.

This day, Sjado, I do not ask for your favor. I demand it.

She wrapped the belt around her knuckles once, then let the rest hang, the iron buckle weighty.

This day, I do not give. I take what is mine.

With these words, the soul of Sjado filled her as never before. Not since the day she'd slaughtered her loved ones in Kundhun. She wished she'd never listened to Afua and gone to the barrow. But she had. And she'd paid the price. Now, she didn't care if she killed another. She didn't care if Sjado was appeased. She only wanted to feel Hathahn's hot blood coursing over her skin.

Hathahn swiped with his sword. Djaga skipped away. He cut for her legs, then drove in with the fighting knife. Djaga dodged, then swung her belt, going for his eyes.

Hathahn leaned out of range, a smile coming to his lips as he looked her over. "The golem must not have given you much trouble. Or are you truly that good?"

In a blink, she snapped the belt at him. The buckle caught him across the chin, sending him stumbling backward. Blood collected along a thin line, staining his short brown beard. "Perhaps you are." He took two quick steps forward, flicking the tip of the sword across her line of retreat, scoring a light cut against her thigh. "I wasn't lying, girl. I will fight you until my dying breath."

Beyond Hathahn, swords clashed: Osman and his dirt dogs engaging Hathahn's crew. There was a newcomer standing at the *Condor's* stern. Afua. She leapt down from the ship but came no closer. She merely watched as Djaga and Hathahn fought.

Djaga felt the anger inside her become something else. She became resolved to what she must do. The furnace in her heart was no longer directionless fury, but a straight-flowing river of purpose.

She slipped the end of the belt through the buckle, and held it like a noose. She baited Hathahn several times. He swiped his sword at her with each one, then charged on the third. She was ready. She ducked beneath his first swing, sidestepped the thrust of his knife. She kicked his knee when he came in too close, then pivoted around a downward thrust. She was a dervish, moving inside his defenses, spinning along his body as he tipped ever so slightly off balance from an awkward, overreaching thrust. Each and every move of her body felt like a prayer to the goddess, prayers that Sjado was answering by granting her grace and foresight and supple movement.

In one simple motion—an act as pure as Djaga had ever felt—she grabbed Hathahn's elbow, lifted it while treading past him in one willowy stride, and slipped the belt over his head. After a powering her heel into the back of his knee, sending him staggering, she snapped the belt tight and dropped onto her back. Her foot against the back of his head provided all the leverage she needed. She pulled hard on the leather.

Her whole form tightened. Her foot turned Hathahn's head to one side. He swiped at her blindly with his sword. He missed with the first but gave her with a deep gash along her right arm with the second. But then his head jerked, there came a loud crunch like the breaking of kindling, and his body went utterly still.

Djaga stared at his unmoving form. She heard only the sound of her own breath, the beating of her heart. Warm blood slicked her left arm as she let the belt slip through her fingers. In slow increments, the rasp of her breath and the thump of her heart were replaced by the rhythmic shush of footsteps. She picked up Hathahn's sword and turned.

Ten paces away stood Afua. She held her hands before her, the way a bride might in the moments before her right hand was bound by a grass cord to her groom. Behind her, Osman and Kaliban approached, but they remained a healthy distance away. They were bloodied and bent. Of the other dirt dogs she could see no sign.

Djaga stepped closer to Afua, sword in hand. The two of them stared at one another, pure opposites, Djaga the essence of battle, of purpose, Afua the embodiment of peace, a woman resolved to her fate.

"Why did you do it?" Djaga asked in Kundhunese.

Afua stared at her, stone-faced. "When you killed our people, I felt Sjado within you. I witnessed the slaughter of three of my cousins. I saw you drive a spear through the neck of my own sister. I watched her die, writhing. And I didn't care, Djaga. I didn't care at all. Her death was like the fall of a leaf from an acacia. Meaningless. I knew I should be horrified by it, but I wasn't. The only thing I felt was an itch, a yearning to get back what I had lost. That was why I left, not because I feared what would happen to me, but because I knew that no one there—not you, not my family, not our king—could restore my soul. That could only come from two-faced god."

"You did all of this"—with the tip of the scimitar, Djaga pointed at Hathahn's lifeless form—"to be free?"

Afua laughed, her dark skin reflecting the deep orange of the sunset. "Djaga! Don't you see? I did this to free *you*! All I've done since leaving Kundhun has been in the hopes of finding a way to force Sjado to release you. You didn't deserve this. *I* did."

Djaga stepped forward. "You *murdered* Nadín."

"And I'm sorry for that." Despite her words, Afua's stone-face expression told Djaga how little she cared. "But Sjado demands sacrifice. You know this as well as I. You've known it from the moment our god took us. You just haven't been able to admit it. But now you can, yes? You can admit it and be *free*."

Afua's smile was mad. It was wrong, and it made Djaga sick to her stomach that she could act so after causing so much pain. Djaga gripped Hathahn's sword. It begged her to use it, as did Nadín's honor. But in that moment all Djaga could think about was how different Afua's toothy grimace was from Nadín's shy smile. How different Djaga's life had been from Afua's since their days in Kundhun. Until now, Djaga had thought Afua cursed in the same way she had been. But of course it hadn't been so. Jonsu, the aspect of peace, had taken Afua as Sjado had taken Djaga.

What would it be like to be cursed with utter tranquility? What would it be like to live life and feel no pain, no anger? Those were necessary for laughter and joy. Afua had been made a husk of a woman by Jonsu. But she was no longer. Djaga could feel it in herself, and she could feel it in Afua as well.

Djaga looked over her dirty, bloody hands. She took in the world around her, the desert, Hathahn's dead form, the ships, crashed against one another like two drunks sleeping off their night at the end of an alley, and suddenly wished she'd never come to the desert. If Nadín were going to die—and certainly that was her sentence; a gut wound like hers could lead only to a slow, painful death—she wished she'd stayed to spend as much time with her as she could. Console her. Usher her into the next world with a kiss, their hearts beating as one.

Suddenly, it was very important that Djaga return to Sharakhai.

Within the medium, Djaga sat by Nadín's bedside, holding the lax fingers of her hand. Nadín's eyes had been fluttering closed for the past several minutes. Her face was pale as fresh milk.

Djaga had been telling her the tale, but had stopped when she'd come to the last. The realization had struck her like a hammer blow in the desert, and it was no less impactful now. Wind and grass, how she wished she could sit here forever with Nadín. Tell her stories of the rolling hills of Kundhun. Have Nadín tell her the tales of her life growing up in the desert with her people.

"Go on," Nadín said, her eyes still closed.

"What does it matter?" Djaga replied.

"I would know before I depart for the further

fields."

Djaga took a deep breath, then exhaled. "Afua wanted release. I could see it in her, all the emotion that she'd been unable to feel since our ritual coming back to her in a rush."

There had been regret in Afua's eyes as the sun had slipped below the horizon, self-loathing as well. More than anything else, though, there had been a bottomless well of sorrow. At the same time, all the rage Djaga had felt over the years was draining from her like water through a crack in a rain barrel. So much had been kept from her, hidden behind an impossibly high wall. How long she'd wished she could truly bask in Nadín's love. But it had been impossible. Her anger had prevented it.

And now it's still impossible, Djaga thought, *just for completely different reasons.*

"*Do it*, Afua begged me, pointing to Hathahn's sword. *Kill me.*" She paused, debating on lying to Nadín. But surely she would learn the truth of it in her next life. "Forgive me, my love, but I could find only pity for Afua in my heart. We'd done wrong, but what our god had done to us was worse. Afua hadn't deserved it."

Nadín opened her eyes and turned her head to look

at Djaga. When she spoke, her voice was a whisper. "Neither did you."

To this Djaga only shrugged. "Perhaps she deserved death. There's still a part of me that wants to find her and kill her for what she did to you. But I denied her. We set her ship aright and sent her on her way to Malasan. She left alone, to find a new life. To find the one she'd lost in whatever way she could."

Nadín squeezed Djaga's fingers. "I care only about one thing."

Djaga knew, but she still asked, "What?"

"Are you *free*?"

Djaga nodded, part of her wishing it wasn't so if only she could have Nadín back. "I am."

Nadín's eyes fluttered closed. A wan smile lit her face. "Then I go with a light heart, Djaga Akoyo, for I have unchained my one true love."

Djaga stood, tears streaming down her cheeks. "You have, my love." As she leaned over and kissed Nadín's forehead, a lone tear fell upon her cheek.

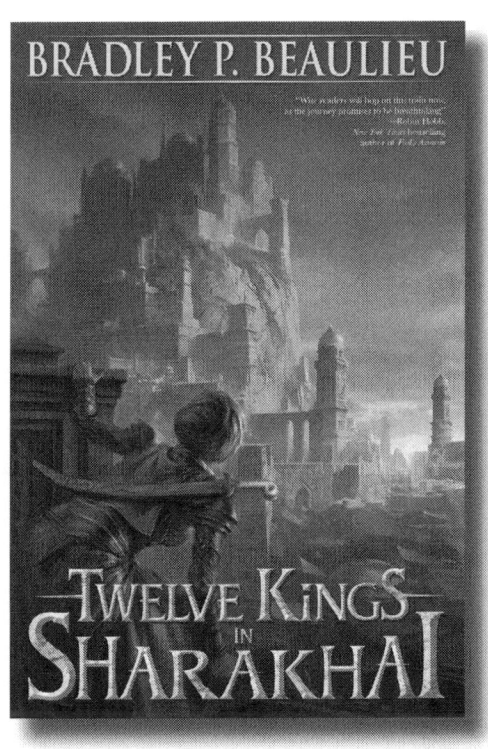

Continue the adventure in *Twelve Kings in Sharakhai*. A sample of the book's first chapter follows...

Chapter 1

In a small room beneath the largest of Sharakhai's fighting pits, Çeda sat on a wooden bench, tightening her fingerless gloves. The room was cool, even chill compared to the ever-present heat of the city. Painted ceramic tiles lined the walls. A mismatched jumble of wooden benches and shelves that had clearly seen decades of abuse made it feel well loved if not well cared for. Were Çeda any other dirt dog, she would have sat in one of the rooms on the far side of the pits, the ones that hosted dozens of men and women. But Çeda was given special dispensation, and had been since winning her first bout at the age of fourteen.

By the gods, five years already.

She tightened her hands into fists, enjoying the creak of the leather, the feel of the chain mail wrapped around the backs of her hands and knuckles. She checked the straps of her armor. Her greaves, her bracers, her heavy battle skirt. And finally her breastplate. All of them had once been dyed white—the color of a wolf's bared teeth—but now the armor was so well used that much of the leather's natural brown shone through. *Well and good*, Çeda thought. It felt used. Lived in. Kissed by battle. Exactly the way she liked it.

She picked up her bright steel helm and set it on her lap. She stared into the iron mask fixed across the front—a mask of a woman's face, cold and expressionless in the face of battle. Affixed to the top of the helm was a wolf's pelt, teeth bared, muzzle resting along the crown.

Echoing down the corridor came a voice that sounded old and hoary, a mountain come to life. "They're ready." It was Pelam.

Çeda glanced toward the arched doorway with the blood-red curtains strung across it. "Coming," she said, then returned her attention to the helm. She ran her fingers over the many nicks in the metal, over the mask's empty eyes—

Tulathan grant me foresight.

—stroked the rough fur of the wolf's pelt—

Thaash guide my sword.

—then pulled the helm over her braided black hair and strapped it tightly on.

As the weight of the armor settled over her, she parted the heavy curtains and hiked up the sloping tunnel into the heat of the noontime sun. The walls of the fighting pit towered around her, and above them, arranged in concentric circles, were the seats of the stadium. *It's going to be a good day for Osman.* Already there were several hundred waiting for the bout to begin.

Roughly half the spectators called the city of Sharakhai home; they knew the pits inside and out, knew the regular dirt dogs as well. The other half were visitors to the desert's amber jewel. They'd come to trade or find fortune in a city that offered greater opportunities than they'd had back home. It rankled that so many came here, to Çeda's home, and lived off it like fleas on a dog. Though she could hardly complain—

A boy in a teal kaftan pointed to Çeda wildly and called, "The White Wolf! The Wolf has come to fight!" and the crowd rose to their feet as one, craning their necks to see.

—the pits paid well enough.

A ragged cheer went up as she strode to the center of the pit and joined the circle of eleven other fighters. The money men in the stands began calling out odds for the White Wolf. She hadn't even been chosen to fight yet, so no one would know who her opponent would be, but many still flocked to be the first to wager their coin on her.

The other dirt dogs watched Çeda warily. Some knew her, but just like those in the audience, many of these fighters had come from distant kingdoms to try their hand against the best fighters in Sharakhai. Three women stood among those gathered—two well muscled, the third an absolute brute; she outweighed Çeda by three stone at least. The rest were men, some brawny, others lithe. One, however, was a tower of a man wearing a beaten leather breastplate and a conical helm with chain mail that lapped against his broad shoulders. Haluk. He stood a full head and a half taller than Çeda and stared at her like an ox readying a charge.

In response, Çeda strode toward him and pressed her thumb to an exposed edge on the back of her mailed gloves. She pressed hard enough to pierce skin, to draw blood. Haluk stared at her with confusion, then a wicked sort of glee, as Çeda stopped in front of him and pressed her bloody thumb to the center of his leather breastplate.

The crowd roared.

A new flurry of betting rose, while the rest of the audience jockeyed for position against the rim of the pit.

Çeda had just marked Haluk for her own, an ancient gesture that not all dirt dogs would respect, but these would, she reckoned. None of them would wish to fight Haluk, not in their first bout of the day. When Çeda turned away and returned to her place in the circle, all but ignoring Haluk, the naked anger on his face was slowly replaced with a look of cool assessment. *Good,* Çeda thought. He'd taken the bait and would surely choose her if she didn't choose him first.

When some but not all of the betting flurry had died down, Pelam stepped out from another darkened tunnel. The calls of betting rose to a tumult as the audience saw the first bout was ready to begin.

Pelam wore a jeweled vest, a brown kufi, and a red kaftan that was not only fashionable but fine, save for its hem, which was hopelessly dusty from its days sweeping the pit floors. In one of Pelam's skeletal hands he held a woven basket. As the fighters parted for him, he stepped to the rough center of their circle and flipped the basket lid open. After one last check around him to ensure all was ready, he shot his hand into basket's confines and lifted a horned viper as long as his lanky legs. The snake wriggled, swelling its hood and hissing, baring its fangs for all to see.

Pelam knew his business, but the snake made Çeda's hackles rise. Bites were rare but not unheard of, especially if one of the fighters was inexperienced and jumped when the snake drew near. Çeda knew enough to remain still, but foreigners didn't always follow Pelam's careful pre-bout instructions, and it wasn't always the person who jumped that the snakes chose to sink their fangs into.

As Pelam held the writhing snake, each of the fighters spread their legs wide until their sandaled or booted feet butted up against each other's. After a glance at each of the fighter's stances, and finding them proper, Pelam dropped the snake and stepped away.

It lay there, coiling itself tightly. The crowd shouted to the baked desert air, their voices rising to a fever pitch as each yelled the name of their chosen fighter. The fighters themselves remained silent. Oddly, the snake slithered toward Pelam for a moment, then seemed to think better of it and turned to glide over the sand to Çeda's left, then turned once more. And slithered straight through Haluk's legs.

Silence followed as a pit boy ran and snatched the viper by its tail, lowering it back into its basket as the snake spun like a woodworker's auger.

Pelam calmly awaited Haluk's choice.

The big man didn't hesitate. He made straight for Çeda and spat on the ground at her feet.

The crowd went wild. "The Oak of the Guard has chosen the White Wolf!"

Oak indeed. Haluk was a captain of the Silver Spears, and a tree of a man, but he was also a particularly *cruel* man, and it was time he learned a lesson.

Like jackals to a kill, the news drew spectators from neighboring pits. The stands were soon brimming with them.

As the rest of the fighters exited the pit, a dozen boys jogged out from the tunnels bearing wooden swords and shields and clubs. Çeda, as the challenged, would normally be allowed to choose weapons first, but she followed ancient custom; she had marked him, and thus *she* was the true challenger, not Haluk, so she bowed her head and waved to the weapons, granting first choice to Haluk. Most would have returned the

honor, but Haluk merely grunted and chose one of the
few weapons meant for both him and his opponent:
the fetters.

The noise of the crowd rose until it was akin to
thunder. Some laughed, others clapped. Some few even
stared with naked worry at Çeda, who had clearly just
been put at a severe disadvantage by Haluk's choice
of weapon.

The fetters was a length of tough, braided leather. It
was wrapped tightly around one of each fighter's wrists,
keeping them in close proximity and ensuring a brawl.

While glaring intently at Haluk, Çeda held out her
left hand, allowing Pelam to slip the end of the fetters
around her wrist and tighten it. Pelam did the same to
Haluk, then took a small brass gong and mallet from
one of the boys.

The pit was cleared so that only Çeda, Haluk, and
Pelam remained.

The doors to the tunnels closed.

And then, after a dramatic pause in which Pelam
held the gong chest-high between the two fighters, he
struck it and stepped away.

There was slack in the fetters, a situation Haluk
would quickly attempt to remedy—his best hope, after
all, lay in controlling Çeda's movement—but Çeda was

ready for it. The moment Haluk lunged in to grab as much of the leather rope as he could, she darted forward, leaping and snapping a kick at his chin. When he retreated, Çeda charged, a move he clearly hadn't been expecting. His eyes widened as Çeda grabbed his clumsily raised arm and sent her fist crashing into his cheek.

She could feel the chain mail dig deep into the fighting gloves she wore, but it was worse for Haluk. He fell unceremoniously onto his rump, his conical helm flying off and thumping onto the dry dirt, kicking up dust as it went.

The crowd stood and howled its delight.

As his helm skidded well out of reach, Haluk rolled backward over his shoulder and came to a stand, so quickly that Çeda had no time to rush forward and end it.

Haluk raised one hand to his cheek, felt the blood from the patterned cuts the mail had left in his skin, then stared at his own hand with a look like he'd disappointed himself. And then his eyes went hard. He'd been pure bluster before, trying to intimidate Çeda, but now he was seething mad.

None so blind as a wrathful man, Çeda thought.

Haluk crouched warily and began wrapping the

fetters around his left wrist, over and over, slowly taking up the slack. Çeda retreated and pulled hard on the fetters, putting her entire body into it, making the leather scrape painfully along Haluk's arm. He ignored it and continued to wrap the restraints around his wrist. Çeda yanked on the fetters again, but he blunted the tactic with well-timed grips on the leather, the muscles along his arm rippling and bulging. He grinned, showing two rows of ragged teeth.

Çeda sent several kicks toward his thighs and knees, attacks meant more to test Haluk's reflexes than anything else. Haluk blocked them easily. She was just about to yank on the fetters again when he loosened his grip and rushed her. Çeda stumbled, pretending to lose her balance, and when Haluk came close she dove to her right and swept a leg across his ankles.

He fell in a heap, the breath whooshing from his lungs.

He grabbed for Çeda and managed to snag her ankle, but one swift kick from Çeda's free heel and she was up and dancing away while Haluk rose slowly to his feet.

The crowd howled again, many of the foreigners joining in, though they had no idea why. The Sharakani knew, though. They understood why bouts like this were so very rare.

Haluk hadn't been defeated in more than ten years of fighting in the pits. Çeda had rarely lost since her first bout, and she'd lost none in the past three years. Everyone knew how widely the story of this bout would be told, especially if Çeda took him in so cleanly a fashion. Few would dare utter the tale within Haluk's hearing, but the entire city would be alive with it by the end of the day.

And Haluk knew it. He stared into Çeda's eyes with an intensity that reeked of desperation. He would not be so easy to take again.

As the two of them squared off once more, the crowd went completely and eerily silent. The only sound was of Haluk's ragged breathing and Çeda's strong but controlled breaths from within the confines of her helm.

Haluk took one tentative step forward. Çeda stepped away, snatching up some of the slack in the fetters as she went. Haluk did the same until they both held a quarter of the length in reserve, leaving them a scant few strides from one another.

Haluk took two measured steps toward her. He was trying to close the distance, but he was no longer reckless. He was cautious, as a man who'd become a captain of Sharakhai's guard *should* be.

Çeda kicked at his legs again, connecting but doing little damage. That wasn't the point, though. She had to keep him on his guard until she was ready to move in. She snapped another kick and retreated, but she could only go so far. Haluk had drawn up more of the fetters, so Çeda released some of hers. Haluk strode forward, taking up more of the braided rope. Which forced Çeda to release more. Until she had none left.

He drew sharply on it, keeping his center low, his balance steady, and Çeda was drawn forward until she was just out of his striking range.

The crowd began to stamp their feet, the sound of it reverberating in the pit, but otherwise they were silent, rapt.

Haluk pulled again, harder now that they were so close. And that's when Çeda moved.

Using the tension on the fetters to pull herself forward, she launched herself with a leap, straight into his body. In his surprise, Haluk grasped for her neck, but she slipped her forearms inside his and grabbed two fistfuls of his lanky brown hair. She wrapped her legs around his waist, twisted them around his thighs, and locked her feet around his knees, hoping to trip him up and end this once and for all.

He didn't fall, however. He was too big. Too strong. And he did exactly what she would have done. He rose up, preparing to slam her against the ground.

At the high point of his lift, she did the only thing she could: she clung hard to his neck and waist.

When they came down, they came down hard. Pain burst across Çeda's back and rump as Haluk's full weight bore down on her. Through her coughing and the ringing in her ears, she could hear him laughing. "Foolish move, girl."

He tried to lift away, but she'd locked her arms around his neck. Her legs hugged tightly to his waist. He was strong, but he had no leverage to break her grip. Again and again he tried to lift himself away from her to give himself room to punch, but each time he did, she began slipping her arms around his neck to cut off his blood. He would drop to prevent it, and then they were back, body to body, breath coming hard and fast, the very intimate duel continuing as each struggled for any small amount of leverage.

Once, when he lifted his head too far away, she crashed her forehead against his. The lip of her helm left a long cut against his skin. Blood seeped down his forehead, along his nose. It pattered against her steel mask, filling her nostrils with the smell of it.

Then, in a sudden and furious move, Haluk lifted, slipping a forearm across her throat, managing to pin her down.

Immediately the crowd was up, shouting, raging. But it all became little more than a keen ringing in Çeda's ears. She heard her own heart thrumming. Felt Haluk's arm tighten further.

It was a strong move, a *wise* move under the conditions, but he'd left himself open. She slipped her right hand down along his left arm, near his elbow, where she'd have the most leverage, and pushed. She let out a guttural cry while muscling his arm up, which had the effect of propelling herself down along his body, just enough to slip her head under his armpit and out of the lock.

He tried to slip his arm back under her neck, but before he could, she grabbed the buckles along the far edge of his breastplate and hauled herself away, and now she was halfway to his back. Exactly where she wanted to be.

She reached her left arm—the one tied to the fetters—up and over his head. The rope slipped neatly down along his face and across his neck. Immediately she tightened her grip and drew the fetters back.

Haluk knew what was happening—he tried to

throw her off, at least enough to get his fingers beneath the fetters—but her grip was too sure. Still, he was a bull of a man. She grunted while gritting her teeth and arching her back. Her arms strained like cording on a ship's sails.

She thought surely he would have pounded his hand against the ground by now, giving up the match, or fallen unconscious, but he hadn't. He still struggled for air, his breath coming out in a desperate hiss, his mouth frothing from it. And then finally, all at once, his body went slack.

Çeda didn't hear the strike of Pelam's gong, marking the end of the bout.

But the crowd she heard.

Their elation could no longer be contained. They stomped their feet. They shook their fists. "The Wolf has won! The Wolf has won!"

Ignoring them, Çeda pushed Haluk onto his back and straddled his chest. She unwrapped the fetters and saw the blood drain from him, casting his face in a strange, deathly pallor.

His eyes blinked open. He stared into Çeda's eyes with a look of confusion, then took in his surroundings as if he had no idea where he was. The roaring crowd and Çeda's masked face soon registered, though, and a look of deep and inexpressible anger stole over him.

Çeda leaned down until they were chest-to-chest and whispered into his ear. "The next time you take your hands to your daughter, Haluk Emet'ava"—she pressed the thumbnail of her right hand into his side, in the depression between his fourth and fifth ribs—"it will go much worse for you." She leaned closer still and whispered, "The next time, it will be a knife in the dark, not a beating in the light." She rose, her legs still straddling him, and stared down into his eyes. "Do you understand?"

Haluk blinked. He made no acknowledgement of her demand, but there was shame in his eyes, a shame that spoke the truth of his crimes better than words ever could.

Like a wedge driving ever further into a thick piece of wood, she pressed her thumb deeper. "I would hear your answer."

He grimaced against the discomfort, licked his lips and glanced to the cheering crowd. Then he nodded to her. "I understand."

Çeda nodded back, then stood and stepped away.

Pelam had watched this exchange with a glint in his eye that landed somewhere between curious and concerned, but he made no mention of it. He merely turned and presented Çeda to the crowd with a bow of his head and a flourish of his hand. As some howled and others collected their winnings, Çeda was surprised to see that Osman himself had come to watch—Osman, the owner of these pits, a retired pit fighter himself, the man she'd had to trick to earn her first bout.

How far we've come since then.

He stood with the crowd on the topmost row. He was one of the very few—along with Pelam—who knew her true identity. She had no idea how long he'd been watching, but surely he'd caught the end. She couldn't tell if he was pleased or not. Çeda gave an exaggerated nod to the crowd, but she and Osman both knew it was meant for him.

He nodded back, then tugged his ear, which meant he wished to speak.

To speak, and perhaps more.

Twelve Kings in Sharakhai is available wherever fine books are sold.

Twelve Kings in Sharakhai is the exciting new Arabian Nights-inspired epic fantasy from the critically acclaimed author of The Lays of Anuskaya.

Sharakhai, the great city of the desert, center of commerce and culture, has been ruled from time immemorial by twelve kings—cruel, ruthless, powerful, and immortal. With their army of Silver Spears, their elite company of Blade Maidens, and their holy defenders, the terrifying asirim, the Kings uphold their positions as undisputed, invincible lords of the desert. There is no hope of freedom for any under their rule.

Or so it seems, until Çeda, a brave young woman from the west end slums, defies the Kings' laws by going outside on the holy night of Beht Zha'ir. What she learns that night sets her on a path that winds through both the terrible truths of the Kings' mysterious history and the hidden riddles of her own heritage. Together, these secrets could finally break the iron grip of the Kings' power...if the nigh-omnipotent Kings don't find her first.

With Blood Upon the Sand, Book Two of The Song of the Shattered Sands...

Çeda, now a Blade Maiden in service to the kings of Sharakhai, trains as one of their elite warriors, gleaning secrets even as they send her on covert missions to further their rule. She knows the dark history of the asirim—that hundreds of years ago they were enslaved to the kings against their will—but when she bonds with them as a Maiden, chaining them to her, she feels their pain as if her own. They hunger for release, they demand it, but with the power of the gods compelling them, they find the yokes around their necks unbreakable.

When Çeda and Emre are drawn into a plot of the blood mage, Hamzakiir, they sail across the desert to learn the truth, and a devastating secret is revealed, one that may very well shatter the power of the hated kings. They plot quickly to take advantage of it, but it may all be undone if Çeda cannot learn to navigate the shifting tides of power in Sharakhai and control the growing anger of the asirim that threatens to overwhelm her.

A Veil of Spears, Book Three of The Song of the Shattered Sands...

The Night of Endless Swords was a bloody battle that saw the death of one of Sharakhai's immortal kings. When former pit fighter Çeda narrowly escapes the battle and flees into the desert, she takes with her the secrets she learned while posing as a Blade Maiden. Foremost among these is the revelation that the asirim, the kings' frightening immortal slaves, are in fact Çeda's own ancestors, survivors of the fabled thirteenth tribe.

Çeda returns to Sharakhai, hoping to break the chains of the enslaved asirim and save her people. She soon discovers that the once-unified front of the kings is crumbling. Feeling their power slipping away, the kings vie for control over the city and the desert beyond.

As Çeda works to free the asirim and rally them to the defense of the thirteenth tribe, the Kings of Sharakhai prepare for a grand clash that may decide the fate of all.

Of Sand and Malice Made, a Shattered Sands novel...

Çeda is the youngest pit fighter in the history of Sharakhai. She's made her name in the arena as the fearsome White Wolf. None but her closest friends and allies know her true identity. But this all changes when she crosses the path of Rümayesh, an ehrekh, a sadistic creature forged aeons ago by the god of chaos.

The ehrekh are desert dwellers, but for centuries Rümayesh has lurked in the dark corners of Sharakhai, combing the populace for jewels that might interest her. Çeda flees the ehrekh's attentions, but that only makes Rümayesh covet her even more. Rümayesh grows violent. She threatens to unmask Çeda as the White Wolf, but the danger grows infinitely worse when she turns her attention to Çeda's friends. Çeda is horrified. She's seen firsthand the suffering left in Rümayesh's wake.

As Çeda fights to protect the people dearest to her, Rümayesh comes closer to attaining her prize and the struggle becomes a battle for Çeda's very soul.

The critically acclaimed trilogy, The Lays of Anuskaya, is now available in an omnibus edition.

Among inhospitable and unforgiving seas stands Khalakovo, a mountainous archipelago of seven islands, its prominent eyrie stretching a thousand feet into the sky. Serviced by windships bearing goods and dignitaries, Khalakovo's eyrie stands at the crossroads of world trade. But all is not well in Khalakovo. Conflict has erupted between the ruling Landed, the indigenous Aramahn, and the fanatical Maharraht, and a wasting disease has grown rampant over the past decade. Now, Khalakovo is to play host to the Nine Dukes, a meeting which will weigh heavily upon Khalakovo's future.

When an elemental spirit attacks an incoming windship, Prince Nikandr, is tasked with finding the child prodigy believed to be behind the summoning. Can the Dukes, thirsty for revenge, be held at bay?

Can Khalakovo be saved? The elusive answer drifts upon the Winds of Khalakovo...

Find more adventures in other worlds with *Lest Our Passage Be Forgotten & Other Stories*...

With *The Winds of Khalakovo*, Bradley P. Beaulieu established himself as a talented new voice in epic fantasy. Now, with the release of his premiere short story collection, Beaulieu demonstrates his ability to weave tales that explore other worlds in ways that are at once bold, imaginative, and touching. *Lest Our Passage Be Forgotten & Other Stories* contains 17 stories that range from the epic to the heroic, some in print for the first time.

This story collection features two stories from the world of The Lays of Anuskaya. "To the Towers of Tulandan" is a prequel story that tells of Nasim's travels with Ashan before he met Nikandr Khalakovo. And "Prima" is a sequel that reveals what becomes of the three sisters of Vostroma. Also included in the collection is a never-before-published story from Beaulieu's Norse-inspired world of Bryndlholt.

Twelve Kings in Sharakhai marked the start of a bold new epic fantasy series for critically acclaimed author Bradley P. Beaulieu.

In the Stars I'll Find You & Other Tales of Futures Fantastic features Beaulieu's science fictional work, from exploring far-flung worlds to finding what it means to be human through artificial intelligence to the cost of dividing ourselves—or ourself—through the use of technology.

In this short story collection, you'll find eleven tales that explore our very human relationship with technology, some in print for the first time.

ABOUT THE AUTHOR

Bradley P. Beaulieu fell in love with fantasy from the moment he started reading *The Hobbit* in third grade. From that point on, though he tried reading many other things, fantasy became his touchstone. He always came back to it, and when he started to dabble in writing, fantasy—epic fantasy especially—was the type of story he most dearly wished to share.

Twelve Kings in Sharakhai, the first book in his latest series, The Song of the Shattered Sands, was named to over twenty "Best of the Year" lists when it was released in 2015. His critically acclaimed series, The Lays of Anuskaya, has recently been released in omnibus form.

Brad, who recently became a full-time writer, lives in Racine, Wisconsin with his wife and two children. Beyond writing, cooking has become an obsession. His favorite dishes are French, Italian, and Mexican/Southwestern, but he is also fascinated by the art of bread baking.

For more, please visit www.quillings.com.

Made in the USA
Middletown, DE
12 March 2019